J. R. R. TOLKIEN
POSTCARD BOOK

HarperCollins*Publishers*

HarperCollins*Publishers*
77-85 Fulham Palace Road
Hammersmith, London w6 8jb

Published by HarperCollins*Publishers* 1998
9 8 7 6 5 4 3 2 1

This postcard book © HarperCollins*Publishers* 1998

 ® is a registered trademark
of The J.R.R.Tolkien
Estate Limited

ISBN 0 261 10365 2

Printed and bound in Singapore for Imago

All illustrations are by J.R.R. Tolkien. Each copyright
line appears on the reverse of the corresponding
picture.

The publishers would like to thank the Bodleian
Library, Oxford University, who have loaned us the
transparencies from their collection of J.R.R. Tolkien's
artwork.

J. R. R. TOLKIEN POSTCARD BOOK

CONTENTS

J.R.R. Tolkien was born on 3 January 1892 in Bloemfontein. After serving in the First World War, Tolkien embarked upon a distinguished academic career, though he is best known for his extraordinary works of fiction, *The Hobbit*, *The Lord of the Rings* and *The Silmarillion*. He was awarded a CBE, and an Honorary Doctorate of Letters from Oxford University in 1972. He died in 1973 at the age of 81.

J.R.R. Tolkien was an artist in pictures as well as in words. In fact, for him, the two were closely linked, and in his paintings and drawings he displayed remarkable powers of invention that equalled his gift for words. Although he often remarked that he had no talent for drawing, his art has charmed his readers and has been exhibited to large and appreciative audiences the world over.

In this collection of postcards his gift for water-colours, pencil and inks, and his keen sense of design can be seen. Also contained in this selection is Tolkien's final artwork for the dust-jacket of *The Hobbit*, and the five colour illustrations from the classic tale.

A fuller examination of Tolkien's artwork can be found in *J.R.R. Tolkien: Artist and Illustrator* by Wayne G. Hammond and Christina Scull.

Bilbo comes to the Huts of the Raft-elves

1 *Bilbo Comes to the Huts of the Raft-elves*

2 *Christmas 1933*

Pencil, black and red ink, watercolour
© George Allen & Unwin 1976
Bodleian Library, Oxford. MS Tolkien drawings 59r

The Gardens of Morning's palace

from The tale of Aramanthia

3 *The Gardens of the Merking's Palace*
   Pencil, watercolour, black ink
   © The Tolkien Trust 1992
   Bodleian Library, Oxford. MS Tolkien drawings 89 fol. 4r

The Forest of Lothlorien in Spring

4 *The Forest of Lothlorien in Spring*

Pencil, coloured pencil
© George Allen & Unwin 1973, 1976, 1977, 1979
Bodleian Library, Oxford. MS Tolkien drawings 89 fol. 12

RIVENDELL

5 *Rivendell*

Pencil, watercolour, black ink
© George Allen & Unwin 1937, 1966, 1973, 1975, 1977, 1979
Bodleian Library, Oxford. MS Tolkien drawings 27

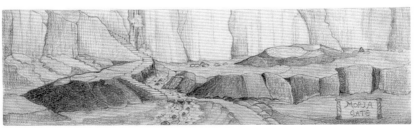

MORIA
GATE

6 *Moria Gate, upper section*

Pencil, coloured pencil
© George Allen & Unwin 1973, 1976, 1977, 1979
Bodleian Library, Oxford. MS Tolkien drawings 72

Moria Gate, discarded bottom section

Pencil, coloured pencil
© George Allen & Unwin 1976, 1979
Bodleian Library, Oxford. MS Tolkien drawings 89 fol. 15

7 *House Where 'Rover' Began His Adventures as a 'Toy'*

Glórund gøes forth to seek Túrin :—

8 *Glórund Sets Forth to Seek Túrin*

Pencil, watercolour, black ink
© George Allen & Unwin 1977, 1979
Bodleian Library, Oxford. MS Tolkien drawings 87 fol. 34r

The hill : hobbiton-across-the Water

9 *The Hill: Hobbiton-across-the Water*

Pencil, watercolour, black ink, white body colour
© George Allen & Unwin 1937, 1966, 1973, 1975, 1977, 1979
Bodleian Library, Oxford. MS Tolkien drawings 7

10 *1932 A Merry Christmas*

Pencil, black ink, coloured ink, watercolour
© George Allen & Unwin 1976
Bodleian Library, Oxford. MS Tolkien drawings 57

11 *The Tree of Amalion*

12 *Bilbo Woke Up with the Early Sun in His Eyes*

13 *Hringboga Heorte Gefysed (Coiled Dragon, with Two 'Flowers') (detail)*

Pencil, watercolour, black ink
Bodleian Library, Oxford. MS Tolkien drawings 87 fol. 37

14 *Taur-na-Fúin (Fangorn Forest)*

Pencil, black ink, watercolour
© George Allen & Unwin 1973, 1975, 1976, 1977, 1979
Bodleian Library, Oxford. MS Tolkien drawings 89 fol. 14

15 *Halls of Manwë (Taniquetil)*

16 *Maddo*

Pencil, black and coloured ink, watercolour
© The Tolkien Trust 1992
Bodleian Library, Oxford. MS Tolkien drawings 88 fol. 31

17 *Mithrim*

18 *Dust-jacket for* The Hobbit, *final art*

Pencil, black ink, watercolour, white body colour
© Unwin Hyman Ltd 1989
Bodleian Library, Oxford. MS Tolkien drawings 32

19 *Barad-dûr*

Pencil, coloured pencil, black and red ink
© George Allen & Unwin 1973, 1976, 1977, 1979
Bodleian Library, Oxford. MS Tolkien drawings 80

Conversation with Smaug

20 *Conversation with Smaug*

Pencil, black ink, watercolour, coloured ink?, white body colour
© George Allen & Unwin 1937, 1966, 1973, 1975, 1977, 1979
Bodleian Library, Oxford. MS Tolkien drawings 30